their pity.

"Come on, try it. It's good! My mama made it." Eli cuts off a little triangle and puts it on my tray.

I eat it. It tastes like blueberries and cinnamon. It tastes warm. Like home. I never eat homemade food.

"Thanks," I tell Eli.

He smiles. "So, how'd you get into heavy metal?"

Maybe it was the pie. Or being early. Or not having detention, but I feel my anger go away. I tell Eli all about my dad and music. And his friend Maurice. And their band "Plantain Sunday." But, not about jail.

## CHAPTER SIX
## Lies

"That's so cool your dad's in a band…and in the NBA!" Eli says.

I nod, uncomfortably. "Yeah. Definitely. It definitely is."

Eli drinks juice from his carton. He is slurping it.

I've seen him humming to his juice box before. I used to think he was a weirdo. But, now I don't. He's open to new music. This makes me like him.

"Want to go see the organ at my mom's church today?" Eli asks me. He tells me all about the Baptist Church. And the organ. And his mom. She's the pastor.

"There's a musician who plays the organ, Mrs. Scarlett. No one else can touch it but her," Eli says. He looks very seriously at me. I nod.

This sounds awesome. I walk by his mom's church on my way to school. Sometimes I hear people practicing music inside.

"I can't," I say.

"Why not?"

"I have to pick up my sisters at school. Then I drop them off at the hospital where my mom works. We eat dinner there."

"Cool! Can I come? We can make a heavy metal band!"

I laugh at this. It sounds fun. But I don't know about my family meeting Eli.

"Uh, let me check." I say.

I text my mom:

Hey Mom, No detention. 😬 Can I bring a friend to the hospital tonight? He's into music. 🎶

My mom texts back:

Yes you can! 👌

I tell Eli. He pumps his fist, "yes!" It's like he just won something.

I'm a little nervous about bringing Eli to the hospital. I have never introduced a friend from school to my family.

## CHAPTER SEVEN
# Kiera and Zion and Eli

O utside of the elementary school, Kiera and Zion wave their yellow mittens.

"This is my friend Eli," I say to my sisters.

Eli takes his hand out of his glove. He shakes Kiera's hand and then Zion's. Zion laughs. She looks so happy. She holds Eli's hand the whole way to the hospital. Eli is also beaming.

At the hospital, the attendant says, "Hello, Jackson family!" She signs Eli in.

Eli very carefully writes his name. He shows

her his P.S. 71 ID. He reads the entire list of visitor rules.

Zion takes her hand out of Eli's. She runs to the elevator. She pushes the button.

Inside the elevator, Kiera, Zion, Eli, and me pound our feet on the floor. Our feet are drums. Kiera and Zion laugh. We get a dope rhythm by the time we reach floor four. The elevator dings. We all yell and stomp one more time and clap our hands. We are already a band.

We walk down a hall. Walk to the waiting room. There are tons of hearts on the wall. One says my mom's name: "Diane Jackson, CNA." Her name is written in curvy ink. It looks happy, too. It's funny how a friend can change the way a room looks. I don't know if it's Eli's jolly presence or what. But everyone in the waiting room seems less sad.

The four of us sit on some empty chairs.

Zion and Kiera get books from the kids' shelf. My sisters like to read books about horses. I don't know why. We have never been to a farm.

Eli and I set up in a corner.

"Let me listen to another Animal Father song," Eli says.

I pull up Animal Father's song "Dark Arms" on my phone.

Eli's feet match the beat. He's drumming his hands on the waiting room table. He's totally absorbed in the music. He looks kind of shocked.

Then he's like, "This is so scary!"

Then he does an air-guitar solo.

My mom walks in. She's got two trays with plates of food.

Eli doesn't know she's there. He's still jamming out to Animal Father.

My mom sits down with a sigh. She says, "Oh, my feet." Then she smiles and watches Eli.

She seems kind of delighted. Kiera and Zion laugh.

Eli looks up, surprised. He takes off his headphones. "Sorry, Mrs. Jackson!"

"Don't be sorry! You're good. You got rhythm." Mom smiles.

"He's like Daddy!" Zion says.

My mom laughs, "A little bit."

"That's so cool that your dad's in the NBA!" Eli says to Zion.

Zion looks confused. Kiera looks angry.

She says, "Our dad is not in the NBA! You tell him that, Jayden?"

I shake my head. "No."

Then I look to Eli. "Well, he's not in the actual NBA. He's in a smaller team that feeds into the NBA."

Eli nods. "That's still cool!"

My mom looks at me. She's waiting to see

what I'll do. We have an agreement. I speak for myself. I make my own decisions. I'm the only one who can figure me out.

I give Kiera a mean look that says, "Be quiet."

She looks confused. She says, "Whatever. I thought friends told each other the truth."

My mom makes a disappointed clicking sound at me. She changes the subject. "Eli, tell us about your family."

We spend the rest of the meal talking and eating. It's taco salad and French fries tonight. And there's milkshakes for dessert.

Eli tells my family all about his mom and his grandmother. He tells us that his mom is a pastor.

"Everyone calls her Pastor Kim!"

Zion laughs. "Pasta Kim?"

"No, Pastor." Eli explains, "She's in charge of our church. We're Baptists."

Zion tells him that our dad is a "bassist." She doesn't know that Baptist is a religion. Bass is just an instrument my dad played.

Eli laughs at this. He takes the last sip of his milkshake. Then he says, "Well, it's 5 o'clock. That's my curfew. I need to walk home. Thank you for the meal, Mrs. Jackson. It was really delicious."

"Anytime, Eli," Mom says. "You text Jayden when you get home!"

"Definitely," Eli says. We trade numbers.

Then Eli says goodbye to me. "See you, weirdo!"

When Eli gets into the elevator, Kiera turns to me and says, "Why'd you lie? You ashamed of us?"

"No!" My stomach sinks. The handwriting on the heart looks sad now. The waiting room doesn't smell good anymore. It smells like bleach and toilets. I feel the anger. In my arms. I want to

yell out. I want to scream at someone. I want to
punch Digby in the face. Digby's not even here.
But I want to punch him anyway.

Mom says, "It's Jayden's friend, Kiera. He's
gonna either be truthful with him or not. It's his
choice. We can't make him do anything. Jayden's in
charge of Jayden."

Then my mom looks me right in my eye.
Like she's trying to see who I really am. Lies or the
truth.

A little while later, Eli texts me:

HOME! Thx 4 tacos & milkshakes

I text back:

No prob.

Eli texts:

Want to work on metal music tomorrow? We
could meet at my mom's church.

I write:

Sure. After I drop sisters off.

Eli texts:

I have to decide what I am made of: lies or the truth.

## CHAPTER EIGHT
## Church Music

It is 5:00 in the morning. I was up all night thinking.

I hate that my dad is in jail.

But, I hate more that I can't talk about it. It's like a curse. If I tell kids at P.S. 71, they'll think I'm a bad kid. They'll think my family is bad. They'll think I'm a failure. They won't even ask *why* my dad's in jail.

It's hard to be the angry kid in a gray hoodie at P.S. 71. I started getting detention before I even started acting out. Teachers just assumed I was a bad kid. If I put my hoodie up, I got detention.

I am lying in the dark. My gray hoodie is on my chair. I see Kiera and Zion sleeping in their bed next to where I sleep. I don't sleep in a bed. I sleep on a couch. I don't mind. I gave my sisters the bed to share.

I am listening to the gospel music that Eli sent me. It makes me want to tell him the truth.

On the walk to school, I see Maurice. He yells out, "Hot coffee! One dollar!" Then he sees me. "How those headphones working out for you, Jayden?"

"They are working good, Mr. Maurice," I say. I smile. The headphones aren't just good. They are awesome.

"Jayden Jackson is smiling! He must have found some new music." His teeth are spaced far apart. He has a white beard.

"Animal Father," I say. I am embarrassed. Heavy metal is the opposite of reggae.

Maurice laughs, "Whatever music moves you, my man, is good music!" He winks.

Then he says, "Hey, if you ever want to drum out here next to me, you could make a few bucks."

"Really?" I say.

"Definitely, Jay," he says. "You got talent and work ethic."

I think about how cool it would be to drum with Eli singing. I bet we'd make, like, a hundred dollars easy. I could buy groceries. I could cook my mom wild rice, chicken, and kale.

"Thanks, Mr. Maurice!" I call out. I run the four blocks to school.

On my way, I keep thinking about how cool it would be to take our music on the street. But, Kiera's right. I can't be a liar. I cannot lie to my friend.

At the Weirdo Table at lunch, I tell Eli about Maurice. He smiles. "That sounds awesome!"

He and I move our lunches aside and write song lyrics. Amy is our audience. Her speech for president in October knocked me out. She's a good poet. She helps us with some of the lines.

"Maci could draw our band logo!" Eli says.

We look under the table, and Maci looks up and nods. I hadn't realized she listened to the lunch conversations at the Weirdo Table. She is definitely weird. But, I guess we all are.

Eli and I decide to name our band "The Weirdos."

"We could make a playlist for your dad's

team!" Eli says.

My stomach sinks. I nod again. And think about how lying makes me feel. Are my bones made out of lies? Is my breath all lies? What kind of person am I?

But, Eli will say my dad broke the rules. That he deserves to be in jail. Kiera's friend said that our dad is a criminal. She said he was a bad person. When Kiera told me this, I told her our dad is a good person. I told her that he is going to be a music teacher someday.

The lunch bell rings.

"Meet you at my mom's church!"

I'm nervous that when Pastor Kim sees me in the church, she'll smell my lying breath. She'll know I am a liar.

"Okay," I say.

"Cool, weirdo!" Eli says and fist-bumps me.

I smile. Eli is always smiling. I think that nothing bad has probably ever happened to him.

## CHAPTER NINE
# Songs Without Words

First Light Baptist Church has big, stained-glass windows. They are blue and yellow. There are lots of seats. Eli calls them "pews." There is a red banner that says, "FORGIVENESS." The organ is huge. Mrs. Scarlett sits on the second floor in a tiny room.

Eli takes me up to the second floor. In front of Mrs. Scarlett's room, there are a few rows of pews. We can see all the way down to the first floor. It's awesome. Baller. Beautiful.

Eli tells me the organ rule, again. "We can't touch it. It's against the law."

"The law?" I ask.

"Well, not the law. But the rules of the church," he says.

This kid loves rules. I know I have to tell him the truth.

We are sitting on the pew. He has the hymnbook in his hand. He's humming different songs. Picking out ones he loves. His voice sounds beautiful in the space of the church.

"Hey, Eli?" I say.

"Yeah?" He's moving his finger down a line of music in the book.

"I told you something that isn't true."

Eli closes the book. He looks confused. He looks angry. "You lied?"

Then he looks scared. "Did we steal that food from your mom's hospital?"

"What? No. That's extra food. The hospital gives it to their employees and then gives extra to the city mission. We didn't steal it."

"Oh, thank goodness." He smiles. "I was worried we did."

"No, that's not the lie. The lie is my dad's not in the NBA," I say.

"No, I know. He's on that other team."

I shake my head. "No. He's doesn't play basketball. He's in jail."

Eli tilts his head. "What? Jail? Why?"

Eli is the first person to ask why.

"He stole money from his job. It was Christmas. He needed to buy groceries and some presents. He was going to pay it back…then his boss found out. They fought. And now…"

Eli looks to the church stage. Then he whispers, "He broke the law."

Eli is quiet. I think he will tell me he doesn't

want to be my friend. Or that I need to pray. I'm not religious. The closest thing I have to religion is music. I think Eli will tell me to go home. I won't even be able to tell him about Maurice. We won't ever play music together. Finally, he speaks.

"Your dad really risked a lot for your family."

"Yeah," I say.

But, then Eli starts crying.

"You okay?"

"My dad is dead," Eli says.

I look at his face. It's covered in tears.

His voice is shaking. "He got in an accident."

His sentences feel brand new. Like no one in the world has ever heard him say this, but me, right now.

"What kind of accident?" I ask.

"He got electrocuted. He was fixing some wires. I got called out of school. My mom was in the principal's office. She and Dr. Waters told me."

"I'm really sorry, man. That's horrible," I say.

"Jail is horrible, too," he says. "Just a different kind of horrible."

This puzzles me.

"You probably really miss your dad," he says.

I nod.

We are quiet.

And we stay quiet. Until the organ starts playing behind us.

It is angry. Loud. Passionate. Awesome. Mrs. Scarlett plays songs I have never heard.

I am not made of lies. I breathe in truth. I am light with it.

The organ music opens my heart. It opens it so much that I hear the notes in a totally different way. Like it blasts all the anger away.

The music circles between Eli and me. As if it is the melody of missing fathers. As if my sadness is mixing with Eli's sadness. Perfect harmony.

## CHAPTER TEN
# Jay

**A** hand touches each of our shoulders. I turn around. A woman in a long white robe and a long red scarf thing is standing there. She is made of calm confidence.

"Hey, Mama!" Eli says.

"Good evening, Elijah. This is your friend, Mr. Jayden Jackson?"

I nod. She reaches her hand across the pew and shakes my hand. "A pleasure to meet you, young man. Elijah tells me you are a very musical person. Much like himself."

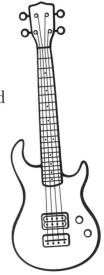

"My dad's a musician," I say. "He used to play the bass with his friend Maurice."

Pastor Kim smiles and nods. "That's excellent."

"He's trying to become a music teacher."

"A noble job," she says. She doesn't ask any other questions about my dad. She is the only adult who looks directly in my eyes as she talks to me. Her listening feels like a deep pond. She is so silent. I can hear myself breathe.

"Come see the organ, boys." Pastor Kim walks to the organ room.

Mrs. Scarlett is wearing a black, flowered dress. She is playing the music. Her eyes are closed.

She sways her body to the music. She plays

like my dad. She creates emotion in music.

When she stops, Mrs. Scarlett says, "Come sit next to me, children."

Eli and I don't even care that she calls us children. We sit down on either side of her.

"Are you allowed to play this organ, Elijah Michaels?" Mrs. Scarlett asks.

"No, ma'am."

Mrs. Scarlett nods. "But, I feel that today is a special day. It is a day of a new beginning."

Eli gets super happy. "It's the beginning of our new friendship!"

I feel my cheeks go hot. This is kind of embarrassing, but it's true.

"Friendship is a divine thing. Magical." Pastor Kim nods.

"Today, I'm going to teach you to play two chords."

Mrs. Scarlett shows us how to hold our

fingers. She teaches Eli the light, happy notes. I learn the dark ones. Together, the sounds twist into each other. Complicated, but in control.

Eli pretends to speak to a crowd of fans:

"Hello, New York City! We are The Weirdos!"

I laugh.

He smiles. "Ready, Jay? One, two, three."

As we harmonize our chords, I realize I don't mind that Eli called me Jay at all.

He is my friend.

And this is a new beginning.

# Want to Keep Reading?

Turn the page for a sneak peek at
the next book in the series.

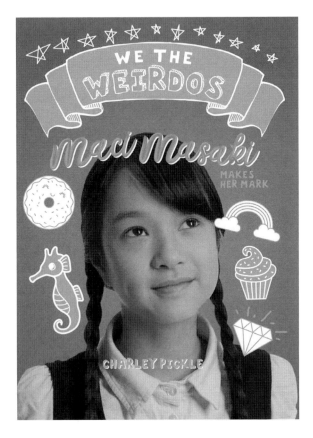

ISBN: 9781538382073

## CHAPTER ONE
## Annoying!

**M**y father thinks I am messy. My mother thinks I don't have friends.

Both of my parents are right.

But I don't need a clean room. And I don't need friends.

My father is standing at my door right now.

"Good morning, Mitsuko." He bows to me. He calls me by my Japanese name. It is too hard for Americans to pronounce. My Japanese name feels like the old me. The one who used to live in

Tokyo. I used to be Mitsuko Masaki. Now, I'm Maci Masaki. I live in New York. I am a whole new person.

But my dad doesn't understand this. He still treats me like we live in Japan. I bow back, but I don't look at him. I am drawing. And I don't want to bow anymore. It's annoying! If I am drawing, I don't want to talk. And if I live in America, I don't want to bow.

"Today is O-souji," he says.

I nod again. I know! O-souji is a Japanese holiday. Like spring cleaning. But I don't know why we moved here if we are just going to do all the same stuff.

# ABOUT THE AUTHOR

Charley Pickle holds
an MFA and is a published
poet and short fiction author.
In sixth grade, Pickle wore a historically
accurate Shakespeare costume to school on
Halloween. Sadly, no one else dressed up.
Feeling rather pathetic, Pickle quickly changed
into inspirational Shaquille O'Neal gym clothes.
Charley Pickle definitely knows what it's like
to be a weirdo and often seeks weirdo friends,
as they usually have tremendously good
senses of humor. Pickle can
be found on Twitter at
@charley_pickle.

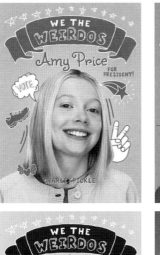

Check out more books at:

www.west44books.com

An imprint of Enslow Publishing

WEST **44** BOOKS™

# What's the Matter with Jayden Jackson?

## Charley Pickle

An imprint of Enslow Publishing

WEST **44** BOOKS™

Amy Price for President!          Maci Masaki Makes Her Mark

What's the Matter with          Eli Michaels, Rule Breaker
Jayden Jackson?

**Please visit our website, www.west44books.com. For a free color catalog of all our high-quality books, call toll free 1-800-542-2595 or fax 1-877-542-2596.**

**Cataloging-in-Publication Data**

Names: Pickle, Charley.
Title: What's the matter with Jayden Jackson? / Charley Pickle.
Description: New York : West 44, 2020. | Series: We the weirdos
Identifiers: ISBN 9781538382059 (pbk.) | ISBN 9781538382066 (library bound) | ISBN 9781538383032 (ebook)
Subjects: LCSH: Friendship--Juvenile fiction. | Schools--Juvenile fiction. | Single-parent families--Juvenile fiction. | Music--Juvenile fiction.
Classification: LCC PZ7.P535 Wh 2019 | DDC [E]--dc23

First Edition
Published in 2020 by
Enslow Publishing

111 East 14th Street, Suite 349
New York, NY 10003

Editor: Theresa Emminizer
Designer: Sam DeMartin

Photo credits: cover, front matter (Jayden Jackson) Arthur Dries/The Image Bank/Getty Images; cover, front matter (doodles) Warja Jones/Shutterstock.com; chapter titles zizi_mentos/Shutterstock.com; series art (emojis) Carboxylase/Shutterstock.com; front matter (Maci Masaki) Plattform/Getty Images; front matter (Amy Price) Digital Vision/Photodisc/Getty Images; front matter (Eli Michaels) Juan monino/E+/Getty Images; front matter (Maci Masaki signature) Very_Very/Shutterstock.com; p. 2 dicogm/Shutterstock.com; p. 12 advent/Shutterstock.com; p. 18 cubicideda/Shutterstock.com; p. 20 Natasha Pankina/Shutterstock.com; p. 24 bioraven/Shutterstock.com; p. 25 hudhud94/Shutterstock.com; p. 40 Visual Generation/Shutterstock.com; p. 51 Mochipet/Shutterstock.com; back matter (seahorse) wenchiawang/Shutterstock.com; back matter (Japanese building) josep perianes jorba/Shutterstock.com.

Printed in the United States of America

CPSIA compliance information: Batch #CS18W44: For further information contact
Enslow Publishing, New York, New York at 1-800-542-2595.

# Amy Price

**Clubs and Activities:**
Class President

**Most Likely to Be**
President of the
United States

**Quote:** "When life
hands you a lemon,
take the lemon and
run with it!"

*Amy Price*

# Jayden Jackson

**Clubs and Activities:**
—

**Most Likely to**
Win a Fight

**Quote:** "Get out of
my face, dude."

JAYDEN JACKSON

ELI MICHAELS

## Eli Michaels

clubs and
Activities: choir,
cooking club,
Volunteer club

Most Likely to
cheer You Up

Quote:"Do the right
thing, and the sun
will always shine
your way!"

Maci Masaki

## Maci Masaki

clubs and
Activities: Art
club

Most Likely to
Become a Famous
Artist

Quote:"I wish
life were in
watercolor."

**weirdo:** a strange or unique person who is often not accepted by a larger group

## CHAPTER ONE
# Detention

**M**y hoodie feels good. Warm. Like blankets.

And, it's gray. My favorite color.

I am at Public School 71. It is 3:17 p.m.

I'm in detention. Again. Always.

The teachers here don't understand me. No one does. I don't have any friends. Not one single friend. But, I don't want any.

I am quiet. Really quiet. I like listening better than talking. I don't know why everyone has to speak so loudly. All the time.

The kids here are yelling. They are loud. They call me names that are not my name.

My name is Jayden Jackson.

Not Jay-dawg.

Not Jay-son.

Not Jay-bird.

Jayden. Jackson.

The only people who can call me "Jay" are people I love. And that is five people: my mom, my dad, my sister Kiera, my sister Zion, and my dad's friend, Maurice. He's like a second dad.

These are the *only* people who can call me Jay. When the P.S. 71 kids call me one of those other names, I explode.

Like a bomb. Like a firecracker. Like a bull.

I yell. Really loud. "THAT IS NOT MY NAME!"

Then, I get detention.

The only good part of detention is that it has a computer. And I've got headphones. Maurice gave them to me. Well, I bought them from him. But the price was so low, he pretty much gave them to me. He's a musician. So, he understands the need to hear music. All the time.

Right now, I'm listening to the band Animal Father. It's heavy metal.

I don't look like I would like heavy metal. But I do. It can go from quiet to angry in one second. I love it. Animal Father is all about control. I put my hoodie up. I sink into the music.

The detention teacher pulls my headphones off my ears. He says, "No hoodie, Jayson!"

I look up. He has a mustache. He wears mega-white sneakers. Like, super white. But not, like, cool white, like LeBron James's sneakers. This guy's shoes just look 40 years old and like they've been washed with bleach.

He is a substitute teacher. He seems like a history buff guy. Annoying. Definitely not a cool teacher. Not like our Life Sciences teacher, Ms. Shelby. She's dope. She's all into apex predators. I don't really care about that kind of power. But, I like how controlled Ms. Shelby is. She can stand in any part of the classroom, and we all listen to her. She's like Animal Father.

"My name isn't Jayson," I tell the sub.

He doesn't listen to me. He just says, "Hood, buddy."

"I'm not your buddy," I say, quietly.

"What was that?" His mustache has little white hairs in it. They twitch like rat whiskers.

"Never mind," I say.

I just want to go back to Animal Father.

I wish I could climb inside my hoodie and come out again when my dad's back home.

My phone dings. The text reads:

Hi baby. You pick up your sisters yet? 🏃

My mom calls me "baby" in her texts. It's nice, I guess. But it's also kind of annoying. She always fixes my hair, too. Definitely annoying.

I text back:

in detention. can't pick them up. 🦍

She texts back mega quickly:

YOU BETTER GET YOURSELF OUT OF DETENTION AND BRING THEM TO THE HOSPITAL. I AM WORKING.

Oh, man. She all-capped me.

"Jayson Jackson! No texting!" The teacher is standing over me. "Third warning. Phone. Now."

He grabs my phone. He walks to the teacher's desk, which is right next to my desk. He puts the phone facedown on the desk. Then he adjusts his glasses and Googles "Civil War facts to impress people." Then he erases that and types

"Civil War facts to impress women." Oh, man. This guy. I have to get out of here.

I need to get my little sisters, Kiera and Zion. They are in first and fourth grade. I picture them waiting outside. They are probably shivering. It's November. It's cold outside. I have got to go get them.

There is only one option.

## CHAPTER TWO
# Run Jayden Run

I unplug my headphones from the computer. I see my phone in its gray case. The substitute has found a Civil War web page. I don't own a winter coat, so I don't have to worry about putting that on. All I have to do is pull out my chair, grab my backpack and my phone, and run.

It's almost the right moment. Timing in music and in life is important. I need to leave detention. It's warm in here. It's quiet. But, my sisters are cold outside. I have to go.

So I do.

I look to my Jordans. Gray. Super fly. Beastly traction. Ready for action.

I pull up my hood. Grab my backpack. And I go.

I grab the phone from the desk.

The teacher turns from the Civil War dating advice and shouts, "Hey!"

Then I hear "Jayson! Get back here."

I don't know who Jayson is. But it sure as heck isn't me.

I am out the door. I am down the hall. I am out the first set of doors. I am out the second set of doors. I am down the steps. Past the panther statue. I am out the metal gates of P.S. 71 middle school. I run two blocks. Past the church. Past the flower shop. The air smells like hot coffee.

The coffee guy yells, "Hot coffee! One dollar!"

He sees me. He yells out, "Any day now, Jay! I know it. Any day your daddy's coming home!" It's my dad's friend, Maurice.

Maurice makes me smile, but it's so cold it hurts my teeth. So, I just keep running.

All the little kids huddle in the elementary school's foyer.

Kiera and Zion are wearing their yellow winter coats. They look like two video game characters with their hands straight to their sides. They are moving so slowly. They keep knocking into each other.

"Yo, Kiera!" I yell because I'm out of breath. I'm tired.

Kiera looks up. She grabs Zion's yellow mitten. They run to me.

"Where were you, Jayden?" Kiera looks scared. She thinks I had to leave them. Like Dad.

"Detention."

She smiles. She's relieved.

"Don't worry. I'm sticking around, monster."
I punch her in her arm.

She punches me back. Really hard. It hurts,
but I don't want her to know that. I just say, "Easy,
Kiera."

She smiles super big. Her yellow coat looks
like a sun.

## CHAPTER THREE
# City of Grace Hospital

**Z**ion, Kiera, and I walk the five blocks to where our mom works. City of Grace Hospital.

"Good evening, Jackson family," the greeter at the desk says. She signs us in. That greeter looks a little like Amy Price from Life Sciences. Short blonde hair with freckles. But her sneakers aren't as cool. "You guys meeting your mom?"

I nod. I don't like talking to people who aren't my family.

I let Zion push the button in the elevator.

She loves this. Zion loves anything with buttons. Fourth floor. Intensive care unit. It's Mom's floor. She's a nursing assistant.

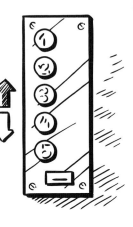

The three of us walk into the fourth-floor waiting room. There are nurses and doctors in blue pants and blue shirts. There are turkey decorations on the wall. The turkey decorations look lonely.

The people in the waiting room look tired. Some look sad. Tonight, one guy's hands are shaking. He's touching his face. When this guy talks, he sounds just like my dad. My dad is from Trinidad. He and this guy have the same accent.

But this guy is asking the attendant to see his wife. I guess she is sick.

I smell warm rice and beans. I look up and see my mom walking into the waiting room. She carries two trays with plates of food.

"Hi babies." My mom smiles at me. "Chicken and rice tonight."

"I don't eat meat, Mom," I say.

"Then just eat rice and beans, baby." Her face is tight with stress. "I'm gonna go get mine."

Her phone rings. The ringtone reminds me of my dad. My dad and Maurice love Caribbean music. Reggae. It used to be all they talked about. Zion is named after some reggae song.

"Hello?" My mom's holding the phone on her shoulder. I can hear a voice through it. It sounds like it's the principal at my school, Dr. Waters. My mom's eyes look at mine. "Oh, I'm sorry to hear that, Dr. Waters."

Her eyes look directly into mine, "Yes, I am disappointed. No, I do not like to hear that, Dr. Waters."

"A student called my son a name. And my son punched this student?"

My stomach turns. Stupid Digby Praxton. He calls me Jay-dawg. It is so annoying. People should not call other people things that are not their names. Ever.

I go totally mute. I put the headphones over my ears. I turn on Animal Father.

But I can still see her talking. She's shaking her head.

Kiera and Zion are eating their food. We are always hungry.

I want to eat mine, but I am too nervous. I did punch Digby. Right in the face. He deserved it.

All of a sudden, my mom is standing over me. I press pause on Animal Father.

"Why are you getting in all these fights?" she yells. "What's the matter with you, Jayden Jackson?"

She keeps yelling, "I have two jobs, Jayden!

I need you. I need you to get your sisters every night and bring them here. You can't be punching anyone! Ever!"

"This kid is awful," I say.

"I don't care about that kid. I care about you. And I care about eating my dinner, which I can't do anymore. Because I had to be on the phone with the principal of your school. Talking to her. Listening to her yell at me because…"

I press play on my phone. Animal Father starts singing in my ears. My mom grabs the headphones off my face. "No. You don't get music right now. You got to earn music. Now, I told Dr. Waters this would no longer be a problem. So, you don't have detention tomorrow."

"Yes!" I say.

"Hold it! I told her that you won't yell anymore. You won't touch anyone. You won't hurt nobody. Not other kids, not your sisters, and not yourself. You gotta find a way to lose this anger you got in you, Jay."

She kneels in front of me, "Your dad is going to be in jail for another six months. This is not going to change. So, you better figure yourself out. Because I can't figure you out for you."

She's shaking her head. I see that her gold earrings are shaking. They have her name in them, "Diane." Her hands are dry. Her lips are chapped. She looks hungry. She has a tear in one eye. I disappointed her. A nurse calls her name, softly.

"Sorry to interrupt. We need you in Room 16A," the nurse says.

My mom nods. Wipes the tear from her eye. She has yellow nail polish. It's so perfect. Except for her index fingernail. It's chipped.

I sigh.

She kisses all of our heads goodbye. She looks me dead in the eye. Stares at me. Like she's trying to see who I really am. A good kid. Or a bad one. A kid who can help his family. Or a kid who's going to make their hard lives harder. She leaves us in the waiting room with our free hospital dinner. Her plate is left behind. Uneaten.

## CHAPTER FOUR
# My Dad the NBA Star

Like I said, I don't have any friends at P.S. 71. I rarely talk to anyone. Except Amy Price in Life Sciences. But, when I do, I tell them my dad plays in the NBA. I tell them he's in Houston. I tell them he's in Las Vegas. I tell them he is always far away because he's such a good basketball player.

They believe me.

Amy thinks it's cool. She told me my dad was like her favorite athlete, Usain Bolt. A champion. A winner. World class. She asked me to tell my dad to get Bolt's signature if he ever saw him. I told her I would tell him.

This is all a lie. I don't want to tell them that my dad is in jail. He got arrested last year around this time. Then he went to jail. I visit him on the weekends. He looks sad and beat when I see him. His face is tired.

My dad says things like, "This is the way it is now, Jayden." He looks like a crumpled lunch bag. But, then his eyes spark just a tiny bit when he talks about music, "Oh my son, when I get out, I'm going to get a good job. As soon as I get out, I got a plan to teach music. I am taking teaching classes in here. These other guys are learning from me! You know, the guitar and the drums! I am teaching them, Jay. Because it's all about the harmonizing. It gives us this peaceful feeling."

But, that's not for another six months. Right now, my family is broke. Like, super broke. That's why I eat dinner at the hospital. That's why my mom works double shifts. And she cleans people's houses on the weekends. And that's why I'm so angry. Everything is hard when you don't have any money. And your father is in a tiny jail cell.

I don't hate Digby. I don't care about that kid. I just hate how he changes my name. My name is Jayden Jackson. It is not Jay-dawg. It is not "Jay-fly the fly guy." It is not "Jay-SON." It is not any of these names. My mom and dad named me Jayden. So, that's my name.

Making friends is impossible at this school. People like Digby make it impossible. I want to explode sometimes. I'm like a firecracker.

And I think the only person who understands that is the lead singer of Animal Father.

This morning, I went to all my classes. I didn't get into one fight. Life Sciences was cool. We are studying islands. I would love to be an island.

Now, it's 11:28 and time for lunch. This means…the Weirdo Table.

I never picked the friends at this table. I started sitting here one day because I thought it was empty. But, then I realized there was someone under the table. She had headphones on and was drawing some crazy-cool pictures. I didn't say anything, just kept sitting there. Her sneakers have little cats on them. They are hot pink and glittery. These sneakers are totally whack. But, she pulls them off. That is how I met Maci.

Amy sits with this happy, goody-goody kid, Eli. He is always singing church songs. One time, he told me I should throw out my hamburger wrapper in the recycling bin, not the garbage. "It's recyclable," he said. He is such a rule-following kind of kid. Kind of like a square. His shoes are red Jordans. But laced very tight.

I never think about recycling stuff. I'm just happy I get a free lunch from the school. I'm so hungry at home. It's nice to have some hot food.

## CHAPTER FIVE
# Heavy Metal Eli

**T**oday, the cafeteria serves rice and turkey burgers. Amy Price is class president. She fought for us. Now we get healthy food. The expensive kind. Organic chicken. Fresh vegetables. Real butter. Real cream. She got us the works, dude.

It definitely tastes better than the sloppy joes we used to have. But, I'm scared it's so healthy that I'll be hungry later.

I get to the Weirdo Table early. It's the first time I don't have to go to the main office.

Usually, at this time in the day, I am being assigned detention. But, not today! It's a new day for Mr. Jayden Jackson.

No one is at the Weirdo Table. Just me. There aren't many people in the cafeteria. It's nice to eat in peace. And the rice is called "wild rice." It's salty. There is fresh parsley on my plate. I feel like a chef on TV. Or someone on a yacht.

We are allowed to listen to music at lunch. I put on my headphones and listen to Animal Father. Animal Father and wild rice. This is living.

A kid waves his hand in front of my face. I look up.

"Hi!"

It's Eli Michaels.

I smile politely. But, then I look back at my food. I just want to listen to Animal Father's guitar solo. It's crazy loud! And good! I feel

my own heartbeat in it.

But, Eli is still standing there. Waiting.

I take off my headphones.

"You need something?" I ask him.

"No!" Eli smiles. "Just wanted to say hi! 'Cause you're at lunch early today!"

"Yeah." I am about to put my headphones back on. But Eli keeps talking.

"So, what music are you listening to?"

"Heavy metal," I say.

Eli's face looks puzzled, "Really? Isn't that like…" he whispers, "…devil music?"

I laugh, "No. It's about injustice."

"Here, try it," I say. I give Eli my headphones.

Eli's eyes close as he listens to Animal Father. He's really listening. Like, really thinking about the music. His whole body listens. His eyeballs dance below his eyelids. His fingers tap the beat. He can feel the music.

Eli takes off the headphones. "I love it!"

"Really?" I say.

"Yes! It's *passionate*. Like the organ at my mom's church. That organ is like a monster. It's so loud. It's scary. But beautiful."

"Sounds cool," I say.

Eli points to the open seat in front of me.

"Can I sit here?" he asks.

"Okay," I say.

Eli unpacks his lunch. His blueberry pie looks delicious.

"You want a bite?" he says.

"No, it's okay. I'm super full," I say. I always say that when people offer me food. I don't want